MINI CLASSICS

SLEEPING BEAUTY

A PARRAGON BOOK

Published by
Parragon Books,
Unit 13-17, Avonbridge Trading Estate,
Atlantic Road, Avonmouth, Bristol BS11 9QD.

Produced by
The Templar Company plc,
Pippbrook Mill, London Road, Dorking, Surrey RH4 1JE.

Copyright © 1994 Parragon Book Service Limited

Designed by Mark Kingsley-Monks

Printed and bound in Great Britain

ISBN 1-85813-665-2

MINI CLASSICS
SLEEPING BEAUTY

RETOLD BY STEPHANIE LASLETT
ILLUSTRATED BY ALISON WINFIELD

Once upon a time there was a King and Queen. They lived in a fine Palace but lacked the one thing that would bring them happiness — a child of their own.

At last, however, the Queen had a daughter. Great was their joy as they held the Baby Princess. Her skin was as soft and as sweet as rose petals and so the Queen decided to name her Briar-Rose.

The day of the Princess's Christening dawned fair and bright and everyone prepared to celebrate the

special occasion. In
those long-ago days it
was the custom to
invite all the fairies in

the country to attend a royal Christening as godmothers. Seven fairies were found and they were given pride of place in the Palace chapel. Little Briar-Rose

gurgled happily in her mother's arms and all agreed she was the most beautiful baby they had ever seen.

After the Christening, the King and Queen and

their guests returned to the Palace for a great feast. The hall was decked with silk ribbons and garlands of flowers. The court musicians played up in the balcony and all was joy and laughter. The table was

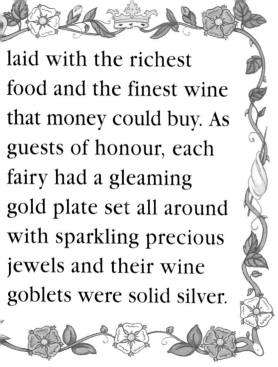

laid with the richest food and the finest wine that money could buy. As guests of honour, each fairy had a gleaming gold plate set all around with sparkling precious jewels and their wine goblets were solid silver.

"Good health!" and
"Every happiness!"
cried the company, as

they held their drinks
high and toasted the
baby Princess.

Suddenly there was a resounding crash and the old oak door was flung open. All merriment ceased as heads turned to greet the new arrival. There on the threshold,

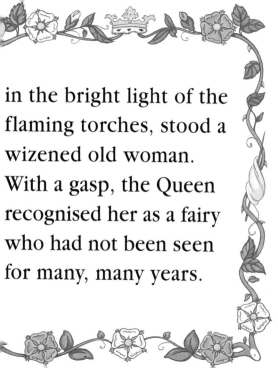

in the bright light of the flaming torches, stood a wizened old woman. With a gasp, the Queen recognised her as a fairy who had not been seen for many, many years.

The ancient fairy
stamped her bent stick
on the floor three times.

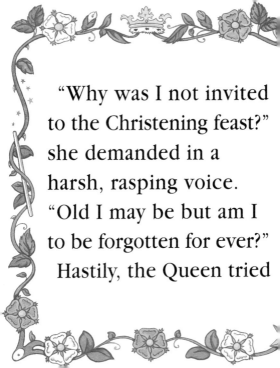

"Why was I not invited to the Christening feast?" she demanded in a harsh, rasping voice. "Old I may be but am I to be forgotten for ever?" Hastily, the Queen tried

to calm her.

"Many years have passed since you were last seen," she explained. "Sad to say, we thought you were dead."

The fairy was very angry.

"I am not dead. I am as alive as the Princess Briar-Rose lying asleep in her cradle," and the old woman pointed a gnarled finger at the baby.

The Queen shivered. A cold chill settled over her heart and she was filled with foreboding.

"Come," she said, taking the old woman's arm. "Come and join our celebrations." Slowly the crone hobbled to a seat

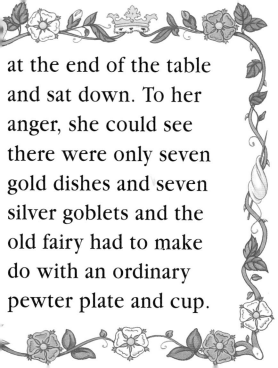

at the end of the table
and sat down. To her
anger, she could see
there were only seven
gold dishes and seven
silver goblets and the
old fairy had to make
do with an ordinary
pewter plate and cup.

She was furious. Loudly she grumbled as the guests made merry.

When the feast was ended it was time for the fairies to give their gifts to the Princess.

They stood in a circle
around the smiling baby.

First, the youngest fairy gave her the gift of beauty.

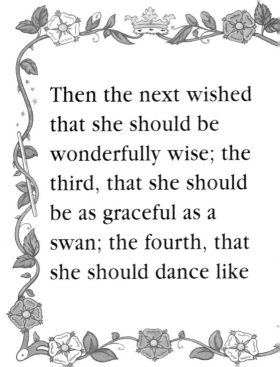

Then the next wished
that she should be
wonderfully wise; the
third, that she should
be as graceful as a
swan; the fourth, that
she should dance like

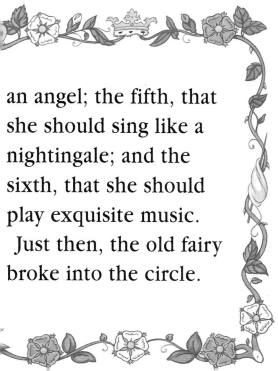

an angel; the fifth, that
she should sing like a
nightingale; and the
sixth, that she should
play exquisite music.

Just then, the old fairy
broke into the circle.

Shaking with rage, she bent over the cradle.

"Yes, my pretty, you shall have a gift from me. When you are fifteen you will prick your finger on a spindle — and die!"

"No, no!" cried the King and Queen.

At this all the company began to weep and wail. Then the seventh fairy spoke. "I have not yet made my wish. I will try to help the Princess but I have no power to undo entirely what my elder has done. Instead

35

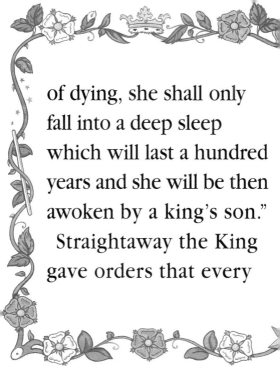

of dying, she shall only
fall into a deep sleep
which will last a hundred
years and she will be then
awoken by a king's son."
  Straightaway the King
gave orders that every

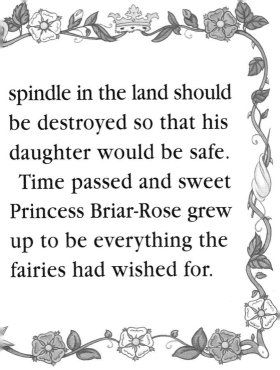

spindle in the land should
be destroyed so that his
daughter would be safe.

Time passed and sweet
Princess Briar-Rose grew
up to be everything the
fairies had wished for.

She sang happily all day long and gave great joy to the King and Queen.

About fifteen years had
gone by since the Royal
Christening and one day
the young Princess was
exploring the palace. She
knew most of the long
passages and staircases
by heart but as she
turned a corner in the

west wing she saw a
little doorway she had
never noticed before.
Behind the door was a
narrow winding staircase
which led her up and
up to the very top of a

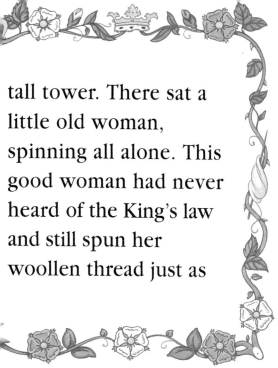

tall tower. There sat a
little old woman,
spinning all alone. This
good woman had never
heard of the King's law
and still spun her
woollen thread just as

her mother had taught
her, using a spindle.

"What are you doing
there, goody?" said the
Princess.

"I am spinning, my
pretty child," said the old
woman, who did not
know who she was.

46

"Oh, please let me see!" said the Princess. "This is very pretty; how do you do it? May I have a go?"

But as soon as she took the spindle the needle pricked her finger, and she fell down in a swoon. The good old woman cried out for help and people came rushing from every direction.

They tried all they could to wake her up, but no-one could rouse her.

Then the King
remembered the old
fairy's wish and knew
that he was powerless.
His only daughter, the
Princess Briar-Rose,
would now stay fast
asleep for a hundred
long years.

He ordered that she should be carried to the finest room in his palace, and laid upon a bed all embroidered with gold and silver.

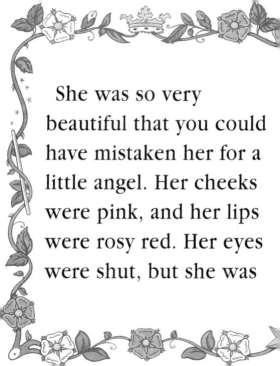

She was so very beautiful that you could have mistaken her for a little angel. Her cheeks were pink, and her lips were rosy red. Her eyes were shut, but she was

heard to breathe softly,
which satisfied those
about her that she was
not dead. The King
ordered that they should
not disturb her, but let
her sleep quietly till her

hour of awaking was come.

When the good seventh fairy heard the news she came to the palace immediately.

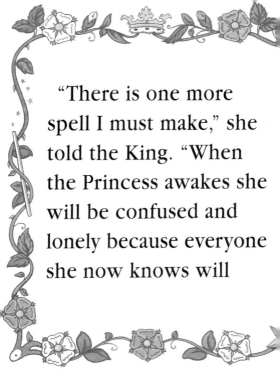

"There is one more spell I must make," she told the King. "When the Princess awakes she will be confused and lonely because everyone she now knows will

have died. So I will put every other living thing in the palace into a deep sleep so they will all wake together in one hundred years' time."

The fairy tapped her

wand on everyone in the
palace; the King and the
Queen, the Maids of
Honour, the Ladies of the

Bedchamber, the fine
gentlemen, officers,
stewards, cooks, maids,
undercooks, scullions,

guards, footmen and
pages. Then she tapped
all the horses in the
stables, the hunting dogs
in the courtyard, the
white doves in the dove
cot and she didn't forget

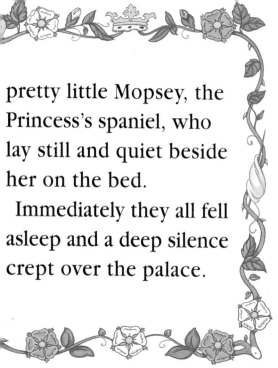

pretty little Mopsey, the Princess's spaniel, who lay still and quiet beside her on the bed.

Immediately they all fell asleep and a deep silence crept over the palace.

In an instant there grew
around the castle a hedge
of trees, great and small,
with thorns, bushes and

brambles, all twining
one within another, that
neither man nor beast
could pass through.

All that could be seen was the very top of the palace towers.

And so a hundred years passed by. Inside the thick thorn hedge nothing stirred.

One day a young Prince came hunting close by. He was greatly

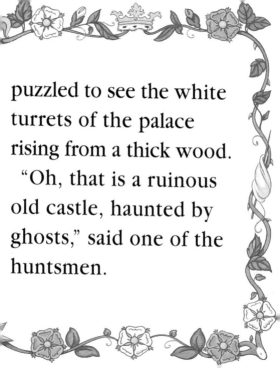

puzzled to see the white turrets of the palace rising from a thick wood.

"Oh, that is a ruinous old castle, haunted by ghosts," said one of the huntsmen.

"That is where all the wizards and witches meet," said another.

Most agreed that an ogre lived there, and that this beast was the only one to have the power to pass through the tangled wood.

The Prince stared at the hedge, not knowing what to believe, when an aged countryman spoke out.

"May it please Your Royal Highness, it is now about fifty years

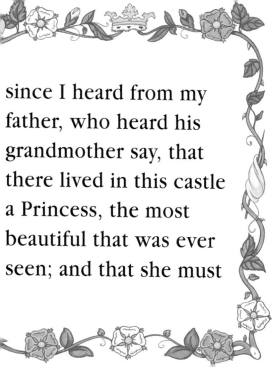

since I heard from my
father, who heard his
grandmother say, that
there lived in this castle
a Princess, the most
beautiful that was ever
seen; and that she must

sleep there for a hundred years, until she should be awakened by a Prince."

The Prince felt strangely drawn towards the tall towers, and without a moment's hesitation, he stepped into the thick thorn hedge.

To his great surprise all
the twisted treebranches,
bushes and brambles
gave way to let him
pass through. Without
so much as a scratch
he reached the palace.

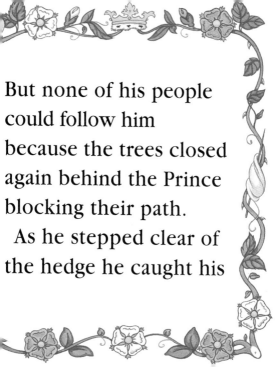

But none of his people
could follow him
because the trees closed
again behind the Prince
blocking their path.

As he stepped clear of
the hedge he caught his

his breath. A frightening silence hung over everything. Not a bird sang, not a dog barked, not a cat mewed, not a child chattered. The brave young Prince walked

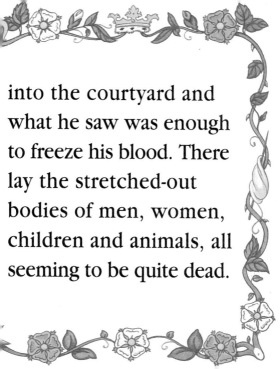

into the courtyard and
what he saw was enough
to freeze his blood. There
lay the stretched-out
bodies of men, women,
children and animals, all
seeming to be quite dead.

But when he had summoned up enough courage to look closer, he could tell by their ruby red lips that they were only fast asleep.

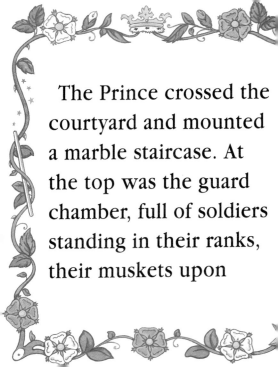

The Prince crossed the courtyard and mounted a marble staircase. At the top was the guard chamber, full of soldiers standing in their ranks, their muskets upon

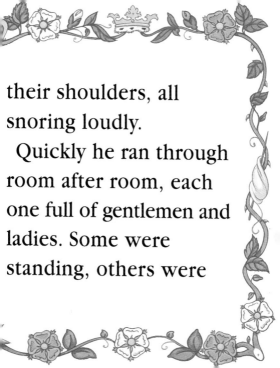

their shoulders, all
snoring loudly.

Quickly he ran through
room after room, each
one full of gentlemen and
ladies. Some were
standing, others were

sitting but all of them
were fast asleep. At last
he arrived at a chamber
all gilded with gold and

there, lying on the bed,
was the Princess. The
Prince had never seen
such a beautiful

sight in all his life and
instantly he fell in love.
He leant over the bed
and softly kissed her.

Now the enchantment
had come to an end,
and outside the window
the white doves in the
dove-cot began to sing.

Slowly the Princess awoke. She looked at him with tender eyes.

"Is it you, my Prince?" she said. "I have waited such a long time for you to find me."

The Prince, charmed by the Princess's sweet

voice, was almost lost for words. On bended knee, he told her that he loved her better than anything in the whole world and would be the happiest man alive if she would be his wife. To his great joy, she agreed.

There was much rejoicing in the palace when it was heard that Princess Briar-Rose was alive and happy.

From a high balcony, golden trumpets rang out and the news of the Royal Wedding was announced. Cheers filled the air as the King and Queen welcomed the Prince and kissed

their new-found daughter.
And loud were the
cheers in the Great Hall
that day as courtiers
and servants alike ate
their first meal for a
hundred years and
outside in the courtyard

the dogs chased their
tails with excitement.
So the Sleeping Beauty
and her Prince were
married amidst great joy
and after the wedding,
lived happily evermore.

CHARLES PERRAULT

The Sleeping Beauty, or *La Belle au bois dormant* was written by the French poet and storyteller, Charles Perrault (1628-1703) and was first published in 1696. The following year it was included in his collection of fairy stories which brought together many traditional folk tales, including *Puss in Boots*, *Little Red Riding-Hood* and *Cinderella* and together they became known as *Mother Goose's Tales*. Written in a simple unaffected style, Perrault's stories quickly became popular in France and later throughout the world.

The Sleeping Beauty first appeared in English in 1729. In a later version, written by the Brothers Grimm, the Princess was named Briar-Rose and the original gruesome ending was amended. Now, instead of the wicked mother-in-law instructing that the grandchildren should be cooked for supper, the story ends happily with the Princess awakening and marrying her Prince!